Theresa Marrama

Treasure Island

Part I: The Curse of Oak Island

TRANSLATED BY ALAINA ARMSTRONG

ISBN: 979-8-9857821-7-2

DEDICATION

To my family who is always there to encourage
and support my writing.

ACKNOWLEDGMENTS

Thank you to Alaina Armstrong for your amazing English translation of this story. Thank you, Valerie Dunning, for your feedback, advice and time spent reading over and editing this story.

Thank you to my brother Scott, who listened as I shared my ideas and thoughts on this story!

A note to readers:

This story takes place on a real island in Nova Scotia, Canada. There have been stories of buried treasure and unexplained objects found on or near this island for years. This story brings you on a boy's journey to find the truth about the island and whether there is treasure there and if it is cursed as many say it is.

TABLE OF CONTENTS

Prologue

There's an island in Canada, in Nova Scotia where one searches for treasure. We continue to look for treasure...

Chapter 1
Another Summer in Canada

"Daniel, what are you thinking?" asks his father.

Daniel is in the car with his parents. He looks out the car window. He doesn't talk. He is silent because he isn't happy. He is more frustrated than ever because it's summer vacation and he needs to go to Nova Scotia in Canada. He doesn't want to go to Canada. He wants to spend time with his friends during summer vacation. But, more than anything, Daniel wants to have adventures with his friends.

"Daniel, I know that you aren't happy, but you can't stay home alone during summer vacation!" says his father.

He doesn't look at his dad when he talks to him. He continues to look out the car window. He thinks about his friends and summer vacation. He thinks about all the activities his friends are going to do this summer. He can't do these activities. He needs to go to Canada. He doesn't have a choice. There's nothing to do there. His dad works all summer. He's a construction worker.

"I'm thinking about my friends and about how I don't want to spend time in Canada this summer," responds Daniel, frustrated.

Daniel doesn't want to spend time with his grandfather. They don't have anything in common. He doesn't want to go to Canada with his parents. He won't have the same experience in Canada because his friends aren't there. His father tells him that his friends can visit him, but Canada is far from home.

"Mom, I'm hungry. I want to eat," Daniel tells her.

Daniel's mother is also in the car. She looks at her phone. She's going to Canada to help her husband repair houses.

"Daniel, we're going to be there in a few minutes, and you can eat then," responds his mother.

Daniel doesn't respond. He looks out the window in silence. He rolls his eyes and thinks, *Why can't my father work in New York for the summer?*

Chapter 2
A Different Discovery

"Dad," calls Daniel. "Where's my baseball glove?"

Daniel's in the attic of the house where he will live with his parents during the summer. He looks for his baseball glove. Baseball is his favorite sport.

Now, he is 15 years old, and he is a very good baseball player. He likes being outdoors.

But more than anything, Daniel likes to read books. He likes to read detective novels. When Daniel was young, he liked to read about buried treasure and mysteries.

Two chests in the corner of the attic catch Daniel's attention. He sees that they are very old, like the chests filled with treasure in T.V. shows that he watched when he was young.

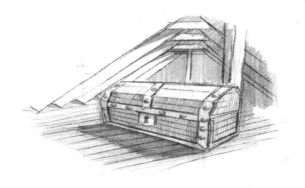

At this moment, he sees his baseball glove on the ground. He grabs it and starts to leave the attic but stops. He turns back to the two chests. He looks inside and notices something interesting at the bottom of the trunk.

It's an old paper. It looks very old, yellowed by time. He takes the paper. He looks at it. He looks at it with wide open eyes. He realizes it's a map. He says to himself, *It's a very old map. It's a map of an island.* He looks at the map and there are two words written in big letters, "Oak Island."

"Daniel what's wrong? How are you?" his father asks when he enters the attic.

Daniel doesn't respond. He continues to concentrate on the map and doesn't hear his father. At this moment, Daniel's father notices that Daniel has a paper in his hands.

"Daniel! What's in your hands?" asks his father in a serious voice.

His father looks at the paper with a serious expression. Daniel hides the map at the bottom of the chest. He closes it quickly.

"It's not important, Dad. It's just an old newspaper I found in the chest with my baseball glove," explains Daniel.

"Why did you call me?" asks his father.

"I called you because I couldn't find my baseball glove, but I found it!" Daniel responds to him nervously.

"Is that so? So come downstairs right now," says his father as he leaves the attic.

At this moment, Daniel looks for the old map that he found. He wants to examine the map. He wants to examine the symbols on the map. He examines it, but he doesn't understand. He thinks about all the possibilities: *Why is there a map of Oak Island in the attic of this old house? Is it possible that I will find secret treasure? Is it possible that there is a chest full of secret treasures on Oak Island?*

"Daaanieeeeel!" calls his mother. "We are going to eat!"

"One minute mom!" responds Daniel.

Daniel hides the map in the chest where he found it. He is so preoccupied with the map that he forgets his baseball glove.

Chapter 3
A Lot of Questions

The map of Oak Island

After dinner, Daniel is in the living room, on the couch. He is watching tv when his dad asks him:

"Daniel, do you want to play baseball?"

At this moment, Daniel realizes that he forgot his baseball glove in the attic.

"Yes, Dad, I want to play baseball, but I need to look for my baseball glove in the attic."

"You found it this afternoon, didn't you?" asks his father.

"Yes, but I forgot it in the attic," responds Daniel.

Daniel goes up the stairs. While he's going up the stairs to the attic, he can't stop thinking about the map. This map is not like the other maps. He's never seen a map like this. He's seen maps at school and on the internet, but this map is very old and very mysterious.

The house where Daniel lives during the summer in Canada is also very old and mysterious. It's a historical site that his father repaired last summer. His father explained that he had found a lot of old photos and old papers when he was repairing the house. Daniel likes to listen to the stories of the house. He thinks this house is a mystery because it's very old. The house was built in 1840. "*The house is old like the map that he found. Maybe there's a connection between the house and the map,*" thinks Daniel.

His grandfather's house is in the village of Chester. The village of Chester isn't far.

He enters the attic, and grabs his baseball glove. He is curious. He wants to look at the map another time. He decides to open the chest and take the old map. He examines it for a long time. He doesn't understand. All of a sudden, his dad calls:

"Daniel! Do you want to play baseball or not?"

"I'm coming, Dad!"

Daniel goes down the stairs and hides the map in his room.

Outside, Daniel plays baseball with his dad. Normally, he doesn't spend a lot of time with his dad. His dad works all the time. Daniel likes when he can spend time with him. He also likes to play baseball with him.

He can't stop thinking about the map. He asks his father:

"Dad, what is Oak Island?"

His father looks at him strangely and says,

"Oak Island is close to here. There's an old legend about the island."

"An old legend?" asks Daniel interested.

"Yes, according to the legend, a pirate buried his treasure on Oak Island," explains his father.

"Treasure buried on Oak Island!" exclaimed Daniel. He couldn't believe his ears. He thought: *If there's treasure on Oak Island, is it possible that I found the treasure map?* He thinks about the treasure. He can't concentrate on baseball. At this moment, his father's phone rings. They stop playing baseball.

Later Daniel enters the house. He climbs the stairs, and he goes into his room. He can't stop thinking about the legend and the information that his dad gave him. He thinks of mystery and pirates. He is fascinated with the idea and the possibility of being close to real treasure.

Chapter 4
The Mysterious Map

The next day, Daniel's in his room. He thinks about his discovery yesterday. He thinks of the map. He thinks of his friends. In reality, he wants to tell everything to his friends in New York. He wants to tell someone about his discovery. He thinks of

Luke. Luke is a boy he met last summer, at the end of his visit. He is the same age as Daniel and lives close to his grandfather. They haven't spent a lot of time together, but Daniel discovered that Luke loves baseball like him. Luke also likes mysteries. Who doesn't like mysteries? Daniel wants to talk about the map. He grabs his phone, and he writes a text.

> **Luke, I'm in Nova Scotia for the summer! I discovered something weird in my house yesterday!**

Daniel looks at his phone while he thinks about the map. Immediately, there's a text from Luke.

> **A discovery? What discovery? I can come to your house after dinner!**

Daniel is more curious than ever. He takes the map and examines it. He examines it for a long time. He notices something strange about the map. The map isn't like other maps because the cardinal points are strange. The cardinal points are upside down. Daniel doesn't understand the map. He doesn't understand why the cardinal pints are upside down. He is curious and he has a lot of questions in his head. He needs to talk with Luke. He needs to discuss the map and the things he just discovered.

While he waits for his friend, Daniel goes into the living room. He wants to talk with his father. He has many questions about Oak Island. He is more curious than ever. He wants to know everything about the legend.

"Dad, do you think there's treasure on Oak Island?" asks Daniel curiously.

Daniel likes the subject of treasure and pirates. He likes mysteries. He finds them fascinating.

"Daniel, I think it's possible. There are a lot of pirates who have visited the island in the past. Normally, pirates have treasure," responds his father.

Daniel thinks in silence for a moment. Then, he looks at his father and asks him:

"Has anyone looked for the treasure on the island?"

"Yes, according to history, a lot of people have searched for the treasure," said his father.

"Has anyone found the treasure?" Daniel asks.

"No, I don't think so." replies his father.

Daniel is fascinated, and he needs to talk with Luke and show him the map! It's 6 at night when Luc arrives at Daniel's house.

"Finally!" exclaims Daniel.

"Uh, good evening," responds Luke, surprised by his friend's enthusiastic reception.

"Good evening Mr. and Mrs. McGuinness," he says to Daniel's parents.

"Let's go in my room," Daniel insists, and the two boys go into his room. Daniel shuts the door. He needs to discuss his discovery with his friend.

Chapter 5
The Old Legend

In his room, Luke looks at Daniel. He looks curious. Luke asks him,

"What did you discover? I want to see!" he says, fascinated. Daniel grabs the map. He gives him the map. Luke looks at it and says,

"Daniel, this map is very old. Where did you find it?"

"I was in the attic looking for my baseball glove yesterday when I saw a chest. When I looked inside there was a paper at the bottom of the chest. The paper was yellowed. The paper looked old. I looked at it. After I examined it, I realized it was a map. It was a very old map, and I couldn't believe my eyes!" explained Daniel.

Luke looks at Daniel. He is more fascinated than ever.

"Daniel, do you want to research the island on the internet?" asks Luke.

Daniel grabs his laptop. He sits on his bed, and he googles "Oak Island." He finds a lot of information on Google. He finds the history of Oak Island. He can't believe his eyes. He shouts, "He's right! My dad's right, there's an old legend about this island."

"Daniel, what old legend?" asks Luke.

He continues to search for more information about the legend.

"According to the internet and the legend, a pirate buried his treasure on Oak Island."

"A pirate!" says Luke, surprised.

"Yes, the pirate's name is William Kidd. William Kidd came to the Island, and he buried the treasure," explains Daniel.

Daniel's fascinated with the information. He can't believe his eyes. He can't believe that he found an old map of Oak Island. Daniel looks at Luke and asks him, "Is it possible that I found a map that could help find the treasure?

"There's treasure buried on Oak Island!" exclaims Luke.

Luke can't believe his ears. "If there's treasure on Oak Island then this is the map that will lead us to the treasure!" exclaims Luke and he thinks silently for a moment.

Daniel continues to search on the internet. He is more curious than ever.

He looks at his laptop and says to Luke:

"One summer day in 1795, a boy discovered a hole under a tree on Oak Island. In this hole he found the

corner of a very old map. This day changed his life forever. No one ever found the treasure, and the map that could help find the treasure buried on the island is long gone."

There's a moment of silence. Daniel and Luke look at each other with wide eyes. Daniel looks at Luke and says,

"Is it possible that the map I found is the map that disappeared?"

"Yes, it's possible, anything is possible!" responds Luke, fascinated.

Chapter 6
At the Library

The next day, Daniel wakes up at 9:30, but he doesn't get up immediately. He stays in bed and thinks about the map. He wonders if the map he found is important. He takes his phone and sees a text from Luke.

Daniel looks at the text.

> **Let's go to the library!**

He wonders why he wants to go to the library. He writes a text,

> **To the library? Why?**

Then after a moment, there is another text from Luke.

> **To look for more information on the island and the treasure. The library can help us find the answers we're looking for.**

The idea of treasure and an old map is fascinating to Daniel. He thinks about yesterday and his discovery. He thinks about how the map he found would change his life forever. More curious than ever, Daniel responds,

Yes, at the library after lunch!

Finally, Daniel gets out of bed. He takes his phone and goes downstairs. He goes into the living room, and he sees his dad on the couch. His dad is watching tv. His dad watches tv in the morning before he goes to work.

"Hello Dad!" says Daniel.

"Hello Daniel," responds his father.

Daniel has his phone in his hands. He searches "Oak Island" on the internet while his father watches TV.

"What are you doing today?" asks his father.

"I'm going to the library with Luke after lunch," responds Daniel.

After lunch, Daniel goes to the library. He goes up the stairs of the library and quickly enters the building. He looks for his friend. Immediately, he sees him. Luke is already at the library. Luke is already looking in a special database.

"Luke, what are you looking for?" asks Daniel.

"Oh, Hi Daniel! I didn't see you. I'm researching the people who looked for the treasure on the island," responds Luke.

"I'm going to get some books. I'll be back, keep looking!" Daniel said.

Daniel searches and searches the library for books about Oak Island. But he can't find any. He's not happy. He wonders: *Why isn't there a single book about Oak Island?* He doesn't know what he's looking for. He needs help. He comes back and asks Luke.

"Luke, did you find something important on the internet?" asks Daniel.

"No, I don't know what I'm looking for," explains Luke.

At this moment, Daniel has an idea. He has an idea that can help them find some information.

"Luke, I want to visit my grandfather. He lives close to Oak Island. He's lived there for 20 years, and he has a collection of old journals about Oak Island in his house," says Daniel.

"Does your grandfather know the legend of the Island?"

"I don't know," Daniel replies.

The two boys leave the library and think about the legend.

Chapter 7
An Important Conversation

The next day, Daniel goes to his grandfather's house. When he goes up the stairs of his house, he realizes that it's been a long time since he visited his grandfather. His father is always too busy to visit his father and Daniel spends all his time outside playing baseball or in his bedroom reading books. He enters his grandfather's house.

"Grandpa!" calls Daniel.

"In the living room," responds his grandfather.

Daniel goes into the living room and sits on the couch. His grandfather is a very smart man. He was a history professor for 30 years in Canada.

"Hello, Grandpa!"

"Hello, Daniel. How are you?"

"Good grandpa, thanks. How are you?"

"Good Daniel, thanks."

"Grandpa, I want to discuss something with you. I want to discuss the legend of Oak Island. Do you know this legend?"

"Everyone knows the legend of Oak Island."

"Is there a treasure map?" asks Daniel.

"A lot of people have looked for the map in the past. After some time, they realized that the map had disappeared forever and they stopped looking," his grandfather explains.

Daniel can't believe his ears. He looks at his grandfather with wide eyes. He looks at him with a serious expression. More curious than ever, he asks,

"How'd the map disappear?"

"The legend of Oak Island is one of the best treasure hunts in history. According to the articles, even Franklin Delano Roosevelt looked for the treasure on Oak Island. According to the legend, there was a man who had the map in Chester. The map is believed to still be in Canada. But no ones for certain."

Daniel looks at his grandfather in silence. He thinks, *Is it possible that I found the missing map?*

"Grandpa is there a photo of the map?" asks Daniel.

His grandfather looks at him with a confused look.

"Daniel, why are you asking me these questions about the Oak Island map?" asks his grandfather.

His grandfather gets up and leaves the living room. Daniel doesn't understand. He thinks, *Where's he going?* He hears a noise and a minute later his grandfather returns to the living room. He has a paper in his hand. The paper is very old, and his grandfather has a serious expression.

He gives him the paper. Daniel looks at him. As he watches him, his grandfather explains,

"It's an old Nova Scotia newspaper. There's an article about the Island and the map that disappeared. Go to page 3 in the paper."

Daniel doesn't say anything. He goes to page 3. He thinks in silence for a moment. He looks at his grandfather then he shouts, "Grandpa, I found an old map the other day. I think I found this map!"

His grandfather looks at him and says, "It's impossible Daniel!"

Daniel doesn't respond. He continues to look at the old newspaper and the photo of the map.

He thinks *I can't believe it. It's the same map.*

At this moment, he gets up and runs out the door and runs down the street towards his house shouting,

"Grandpa, I'm coming back! You need to see the map I found! It's the same map! I'm sure it's the same map!

His grandfather looks at him and doesn't understand what's happening.

Chapter 8
An Impossible Connection

"Daniel!" calls his grandfather 30 minutes later outside of his bedroom.

Daniel is surprised to hear his grandfather's voice.

"Is that you grandpa? Is everything ok?" asks Daniel.

Daniel's in his bedroom, and he has the map in his hands. His grandfather drove to his house as soon as he left screaming.

"Yes, but I am a little worried. You left my house very quickly," responds his grandfather.

He approaches him. At this moment, he sees the map in Daniel's hands. He can't believe his eyes. He takes it from Daniel's hands. He looks at it for a long time without saying anything.

"Daniel, where did you find this map?" he asks him in a serious voice.

Daniel looks at him and responds,

"I found it in the attic the other day, while I was looking for my baseball glove. It was at the bottom of a chest in the attic."

"Does your father know that you have this map?" asks his grandfather.

"No, he doesn't know anything."

"Daniel, we have to go to my house. We have a lot of things to discuss," says his grandfather.

Together, they go down the stairs and get into his grandfather's car. Daniel looks out the window in silence. He can see that his grandfather is interested in the map, but he doesn't understand why. "What does his grandfather need to discuss with him?" he asks himself. He is more curious than ever. Maybe this summer will be interesting after all!

Chapter 9
An Unforgettable Conversation

"Grandpa, did you look for the treasure?" asks Daniel, very interested in the conversation.

Both are seated at the kitchen table, in his grandfather's house.

"Daniel, I was very young, but yes, I looked for the treasure on Oak Island with my friends. We collected all the newspapers over the years. We researched all the possible information to understand the legend of the island."

"Grandpa, I want to understand this legend. I want to understand why people believe there's real treasure on the island," explains Daniel in a serious voice.

At this moment, his grandfather gets up and walks towards a closet in the living room. Daniel notices that his father looks a lot like his grandfather. His father is tall like him.

A minute later, his grandfather returns with an old box in his hands. He opens the box, and inside there are a lot of old newspapers and old papers. His grandfather opens a particular notebook. The notebook is old and there are a lot of notes written on the pages with diagrams and symbols. Then, he starts to explain everything.

"Daniel, it's important that you understand that there's a special curse on the island. It's the "Curse of Oak Island," and there are millions of people that think this curse exists. People want to find the map that can find the treasure that is buried on the island. It's a very important treasure because there's a connection with the treasure on the island and the jewel of Marie-Antoinette that was lost during the French Revolution."

"People never found the jewel of Marie-Antoinette? Who was Marie-Antoinette?" asks Daniel.

"Marie-Antoinette was the queen of France during the French Revolution. No, the jewel of Marie-Antoinette is still lost to this day. Another theory is that the Grail, a religious object, was buried on the island along with other documents and important treasure."

"Which important documents?"

"It is believed that Shakespeare's manuscripts are buried on the island."

Daniel is so interested in the news that he doesn't realize at first that his phone is ringing. Once he finally realizes it is ringing he looks at his phone, it's his mom.

"Hello, Mom."

"Hello, Daniel. Where are you? At grandpa's house?"

"Yes, I'm at grandpa's house."

"Are you hungry? Do you want to come back and eat?"

"No, I'm not hungry. I can eat after. Thank you, bye."

"Daniel, you need to eat. Go back home for dinner. We can continue our conversation later," says his grandfather.

Daniel doesn't want to go. He doesn't want to eat. He wants to hear more about the legend.

"Grandpa, I can eat after. I'm not hungry. I want to hear more about the legend and the curse. But I don't understand why there's a curse."

"According to the legend, 7 people will die before the treasure can be found. 6

people have already died while looking for the treasure," explains his grandfather.

Daniel doesn't respond immediately. He is fascinated with the legend. He can't believe it.

"Six people have died on the island?" he asks in a serious voice.

His grandfather gives him an old newspaper. Daniel takes it and notices the big letters on the newspaper:

Another dead without treasure on Oak Island.

He takes a moment to read the article. When he finishes reading, he looks at his grandfather curiously.

"Grandpa, why do you know all this information about the island and the legend? I don't understand," asks Daniel.

"The legend and the things that some people have discovered interest me a lot and I have done a lot of research" explains his grandfather.

"What did they discover?" asks Daniel in a curious voice.

"We discovered some silver coins and small old objects. It is believed to be a small part of the pirates' treasure. There are some people who believe that..."

His grandfather stops talking. He stays silent for a moment and then Daniel says,

"Grandpa, what's wrong?"

His grandpa doesn't respond. He doesn't respond. He seems to be in a trance. Finally, he takes the map that Daniel found. Daniel notices that his hands are shaking. His hands are shaking a lot.

He looks at him and says in a serious voice,

"I haven't talked about the legend and the curse in a long time."

Daniel watches his grandfather in silence. He doesn't talk. His grandfather doesn't talk. Daniel thinks, *Why didn't I talk to my grandfather more? He is an interesting man with an interesting past as well.* His grandfather says to him,

"Daniel, there are more things to discuss but I'm tired. You can come back tomorrow, and we can continue this conversation."

"Yes, I understand Grandpa," says Daniel.

Daniel walks towards the door when his grandfather says to him,

"Daniel, don't tell anyone about the map."

Daniel opens the door, and at that moment he realizes that his grandfather knows more about the legend than what he had said.

As he walks, it is very dark. There's no one outside. There is only Daniel and the night. There's not a car in sight. All of the sudden, Daniel hears a noise. He stops in fear. He notices a shadow. It's a shadow close to his house. He yells, "Dad, is that you?" but the person doesn't respond. Daniel doesn't understand. All of a sudden, the shadow runs. The shadow runs towards the road, and it disappears into the darkness.

Daniel wonders, *who was near the house? Why is someone out so late at night? It's weird!*

Chapter 10
The Long Night

After seeing the mysterious person, Daniel comes home and thinks about the map, his grandfather, and the mysterious person outside. He thinks a lot. Daniel is confused. He doesn't understand why he didn't spend more time with his grandfather. He doesn't understand how his grandfather knows so much information about the map and the curse on the island. In the past, his grandfather didn't seem like he wanted to talk much. After he saw the map that he found, his grandfather looked like he wanted to talk. Because of this, Daniel thinks there's a more important story, a story that Daniel wants to understand... a story that he wants his grandfather to tell him. He's going up the stairs when he hears a voice, his father's voice.

"Daniel, is it you?" his father asks him.

"Yes, it's me Dad," Daniel responds.

"Are you hungry? I bought a pizza for dinner, but you were at your grandfather's house."

"No, I'm not hungry Dad," Daniel says to him, lost in his thoughts.

"Daniel, are you okay?" his father asks him.

"Yes Dad, I'm okay," Daniel responds.

"Okay, what are you going to do tomorrow? Something interesting? Are you going to spend time with Luke?" asks his father. There's a moment of silence.

"No, Dad; tomorrow I'm going to visit grandpa," Daniel responds.

His Dad is confused. He doesn't understand. He looks at Daniel with a confused look. His father thinks, *He's going to spend time with his grandfather? Maybe they're talking about baseball. Hmmmmm...*

It's 10:30 pm and Daniel is tired. He goes to bed. The night doesn't pass quickly. Time passes slowly. Daniel's in his bed with his eyes open. He doesn't think about anything other than the map and the conversation that he had with his grandfather today. Because of this, he can't sleep. He tries to sleep but he can't. He is lost in his thoughts.

Daniel is very tired. He is so tired that he wants this long night to finally end and the mystery of the map to be solved.

Chapter 11
A Decision

The next day, Daniel wakes up early. He wakes up because he hears something. The voice of his father. His father is on the phone and is talking loudly. He goes down the stairs when he sees his father at the table. He is angry and Daniel doesn't understand why. When he goes into the kitchen, he says to him,

"Hello, Dad."

"Hello, Daniel," responds his father, a little angry.

"How are you, Dad? You seem angry," Daniel says to him.

"No. Someone destroyed my car last night. When you came home from your grandfather's, did you see anyone near my car?" asks his father. Daniel thinks for a moment. All of a sudden, he remembers. He looks at his father with wide eyes.

"Yes, Dad, I saw something last night. I saw a shadow near the house. I thought it was you, but when I yelled, no one responded. The person ran in the other direction," Daniel explains. "I didn't see the person because it was dark, but I'm sure I saw someone near the house last night."

"Daniel, why didn't you tell me last night?" his father asks seriously.

"I don't know, Dad. I'm sorry," Daniel explains.

"I'm going to call the police. I can explain to them that you saw someone last night. It's possible that the police will want to talk to you."

"Yes, I understand Dad. I'm going to Grandpa's house if you need me today."

A few minutes pass and Daniel goes to his grandfather's house. When he goes into the house he yells,

"Grandpa!"

No one responds. Daniel goes into the kitchen, but his grandfather isn't there. On the table, there's a picture. In this picture, there are 3 men. A tall man with a soda in his hand, another man with a shovel in his hand and he looks closer at the picture, and he sees his grandfather with something in his hand. It's a paper. Daniel takes a closer look at the picture. He yells, "The map... He has the map!"

At that moment, he hears a voice. It's his grandfather. Daniel has the picture in his hands and his mouth is wide open! He is surprised!

"Daniel, I didn't hear you come in"

His grandfather sees the picture and he looks at Daniel seriously.

"Grandpa, I don't understand. You have the map in this picture, the map that I found. You know, it's the map that disappeared."

At this moment, his grandfather takes the picture and says to him,

"Daniel, there's a lot to discuss. But, yes. I know more about the map you found. Yes, it's the map that disappeared...."

ABOUT THE AUTHOR

Theresa Marrama is a French teacher in northern New York. She has been teaching French to middle and high school students since 2007. She is also the author of many language learner novels and has also translated a variety of Spanish comprehensible readers into French. She enjoys teaching with Comprehensible Input and writing comprehensible stories for language learners.

Her books include:
Une Obsession dangereuse, which can be purchased at
www.fluencymatters.com

Her French books on Amazon include:
Une disparition mystérieuse
L'île au trésor:
Première partie: La malédiction de l'île Oak
L'île au trésor:
Deuxième partie: La découverte d'un secret
La lettre
Léo et Anton

La Maison du 13 rue Verdon
Mystère au Louvre
Perdue dans les catacombes
Les chaussettes de Tito
L'accident
Kobe - Naissance d'une légende
Kobe - Naissance d'une légende (au passé)
Le Château de Chambord : Première partie :
Secrets d'une famille
Le Château de Chambord : Deuxième partie :
Les découvertes incroyables
Zeinixx
La leçon de chocolat
Un secret de famille
Rhumus à Paris
Rhumus se cache à Paris

Her Spanish books on Amazon include:
La ofrenda de Sofía
Una desaparición misteriosa
Luis y Antonio
La Carta
La casa en la calle Verdón
La isla del tesoro:Primera parte: La maldición
de la isla Oak
La isla del tesoro: Segunda parte: El
descubrimiento de un secreto
Misterio en el museo
Los calcetines de Naby
El accidente
Kobe - El nacimiento de una leyenda (en
tiempo presente)
Kobe - El nacimiento de una leyenda (en
tiempo pasado)

La lección del chocolate
Un secreto de familia
Rhumus en Madrid
Rhumus se esconde en Madrid

Her German books on Amazon include:

Leona und Anna
Geräusche im Wald
Der Brief
Nachts im Museum
Die Stutzen von Tito
Der Unfall
Kobe - Geburt einer Legende
Kobe - Geburt einer Legende (Past Tense)
Das Haus Nummer 13
Schokolade
Avas Tagebuch
Rhumus en Berlin
Verschollen in den Katakomben

Her Italian books on Amazon include:

Luigi e Antonio
I calzini di Naby
Rhumus a Roma

Check out Theresa's website for more resources and materials to accompany her books:

www.compellinglanguagecorner.com

Check out her Digital E-Books:
www.digilangua.co